A Gift For:

....

From:

....

How to Use Your Interactive Story Buddy®:

1. Activate your Story Buddy by pressing the "On / Off" button on the ear.
2. Read the story aloud in a quiet place. Speak in a clear voice when you see the highlighted phrases.
3. Listen to your Story Buddy respond with several different phrases throughout the book.

Clarity and speed of reading affect the way Pooh responds.
He may not always respond to young children.

Watch for even more Interactive Story Buddy characters.
For more information, visit us on the Web at Hallmark.com/StoryBuddy.

Copyright © 2013 Disney Enterprises, Inc.

Published by Hallmark Gift Books,
a division of Hallmark Cards, Inc.,
Kansas City, MO 64141
Visit us on the Web at Hallmark.com.

Editorial Director: Carrie Bolin
Editor: Megan Langford
Art Director: Chris Opheim
Designer: Mark Voss
Production Designer: Bryan Ring

ISBN: 978-1-59530-968-6
1PSB2125
Printed and bound in China
JUN13

Hallmark's **I Reply Technology** brings your Story Buddy® to life! When you read the key phrases out loud, your Story Buddy gives a variety of responses, so each time you read feels as magical as the first.

BOOK 1

Winnie the Pooh

Pooh and the Smackerel of Cake

BY **LINDA STATEN** ILLUSTRATED BY **MARIO CORTES, KEIKO MURAYAMA, AND ELENA NAGGI**

Winnie the Pooh woke up early one morning. "Think, think, think," he said to himself. "I'm thinking that I'm forgetting something special about today."

Suddenly, Pooh heard someone, or rather two someones, knocking on his door.

"Good morning, Pooh," said Roo.

"Do you know what day it is?" asked Kanga.

"Why, I believe it's today," said Pooh. "Isn't it?"

Kanga smiled and shook her head. Pooh thought and thought, but he just could not remember.

"Today is Piglet's birthday," Kanga reminded him.

"Oh, yes!" Pooh replied. "That is what I forgot to remember."

"Would you like to bake a cake for Piglet together?" asked Kanga.

Pooh clapped his paws.

Then he said, "Piglet is one of my favorite friends and birthdays are some of my favorite days. We should bake him a haycorn cake."

"I want to help!" Roo said excitedly.

As Pooh, Kanga, and Roo gathered haycorns, Pooh invented a little cake hum.

Haycorns, haycorns are sure to make
a perfectly Piglety birthday cake.

Pooh placed the bowl full of haycorns on his table.
He watched as Kanga added honey, flour, and two eggs to the bowl.
"Might it need just a smidgen more honey?" Pooh asked.

Kanga added a smidge more. The batter smelled delicious.

"I feel a bit rumbly in my tumbly," Pooh said. "Perhaps I'll just have
a little smackerel." So he had one . . . and then another. Just to make sure.
"Maybe a little more honey?" he said hopefully.

Kanga stirred in another dollop of honey and placed the cake in the oven. Not knowing how long a cake should be baked, Pooh sat down and waited.

When the cake looked like a cake should look after baking,
Pooh put it on a pretty plate and covered it with honey frosting.

"Why, Pooh," said Kanga, "what a wonderful job you've done!
Piglet is going to love his birthday cake."

Pooh blushed. "Thank you, Kanga," he said.

It wasn't long before Owl stopped by. He helped Pooh write
HAPY BRTHDA PGLET on top of the cake.

Then Pooh, Owl, Kanga, and Roo headed for Piglet's house.

Pooh felt very happy.

They met Tigger along the way.

"Hoo-hoo-hoo-hoo! Tiggers love birthdays!" he shouted. Tigger was so excited, he could not stop bouncing.

Suddenly, Tigger bounced the cake right out of Pooh's paws and straight up in the air. It landed with a plop right back on the plate.

"Why, I never knew cakes could fly," Pooh said. Everything happened so fast. It was all rather confusing.

There, on top of the cake, was a little nest, shaken from a tree limb.

"A cake should be sweet, but it shouldn't tweet," Tigger said. "Besides, a little bird never stops a tigger."

After Tigger bounced the nest back into the tree, Pooh tried to smooth all the messy spots from Piglet's cake. As he did, he had a nibble just to make sure it still tasted right for Piglet.

Then Pooh stared at the plate. How strange! The cake was shrinking!

The friends began to walk to Piglet's house once more with Pooh Bear leading the way.

As they walked, Tigger wondered, "Uh, Pooh? Did you decorate the cake with bumbly bees?" Tigger scratched his head.

Pooh looked down. Bumblebees were standing right in the middle of Piglet's cake.

"Please go away, bees," Pooh said. As he tried to shoo them off, his paw landed right in the cake. "Oh, dear!" Pooh exclaimed. "I'm afraid I've made a bit of a mess."

Pooh wiped away all the crumbly parts from the cake. Now there seemed to be a lot of plate and not much cake. It really was true—the cake was shrinking!

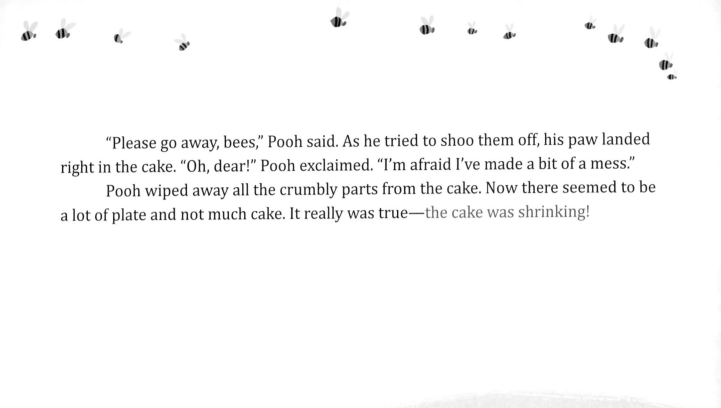

As they strolled along, the wind grew blustery. The plate tipped, and the cake almost fell to the ground.

"Look, Piglet's cake is crooked now!" said Roo.

"Oh, bother. This won't do at all," sighed Pooh.

As they walked up to Piglet's door, Pooh tried and tried to straighten the lopsided cake, but each time he did, more cake and frosting stuck to his paws. He licked them off and looked at the pretty plate. All the cake was gone!

Rabbit and Eeyore arrived at Piglet's house just as everyone else did.

"Nice plate. Very flat," Eeyore said.

"It would look better with a carrot cake on it, though," Rabbit added.

Piglet opened his door.

"Surprise!" all the friends shouted.

Pooh held out the empty plate. "We baked this for you. Only now it's a bit more like an empty plate than a haycorn cake. Are you very disappointed, Piglet?"

Piglet stretched out his arms to Pooh. "Birthday cakes are nice,"
he said with a smile, "but birthday hugs are the nicest!"

"Thank you for understanding," Pooh whispered to Piglet.

"No, Pooh," said Piglet. "Thank *you* for being my friend."

And with that, all the friends gathered around for a great big hug.

If you had fun reading with Pooh, we would love to hear from you.

Please send your comments to:

Hallmark Book Feedback

P.O. Box 419034

Mail Drop 215

Kansas City, MO 64141

Or e-mail us at:

booknotes@hallmark.com